Twinkletoes
and the Burglars
by Berni Hellier

ACKNOWLEDGMENTS

Thanks to the very talented illustrator Mariya Stoyanova for making Twinkletoes real.

Also thanks to Sherry Christie for formatting the book.

Finally, thanks to Rachel Inbar for helping to edit the book.

DEDICATION

This book is dedicated to my Dad who inspired my love of stories.

When my children were little, he created Pixie, an invisible garden fairy.

Pixie left lots of sweets in the garden for my children.

Pixie was the inspiration behind Twinkletoes.

'Children see the magic in the world'

Berni Hellier

Twinkletoes the fairy lives at the bottom of the garden in her tree house with Merlin the Owl.

Twinkletoes is special.

Twinkletoes is magic.

Only children and animals can see Twinkletoes. To grown-ups, Twinkletoes is invisible.

When Twinkletoes gets angry, her feet light up and sparks begin to fly!

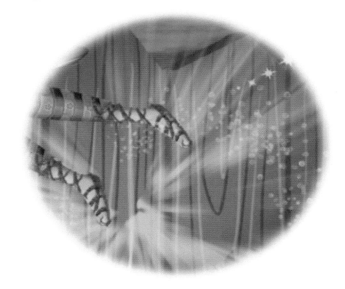

One dark winter's night, Twinkletoes was awoken by whispering.

Fairies have really good hearing.

She sat up quickly, stretched her wings and squinted her eyes.

Near the backdoor of the house, Twinkletoes saw two men carrying big black bags.

Burglars!

One was as round as a ball, the other as thin as a rope.

Twinkletoes watched as the men cut a hole in the back door and climbed into the house.

Soon the burglars came out of the house. Their bags bulged with stolen goods.

Twinkletoes was furious!

Her feet began to glow.

Sparks began to fly.

The whole garden lit up.

Twinkletoes flew up to one of the burglars and flapped her wings frantically in his face.

The burglar felt her but could not see her.

'Pesky flies,' moaned the burglar as he whacked poor Twinkletoes away from his face.

Twinkletoes was stunned and landed on the floor.

Twinkletoes knew that she needed help.

She flew over the fence into the garden next door.

At the end of the garden was a large dog kennel.

In it was the ugliest, scariest dog you have ever seen.

His name was Chief.

He had two ropes of saliva hanging from each chop.

Twinkletoes unlocked Chief's chain, told him about the burglars, and begged him to help.

Now, he looked like a scary dog, but really he was a big softy.

He agreed to help and with one huge leap, he pounced over the fence.

He saw the burglars and gave his scariest growl.

The burglars looked at Chief in fear.

At first, they froze in place, but then, they tried to climb over the fence.

Chief pounced on the bigger burglar and took a bite out of his trousers.

The burglar let out a loud yell.

16

Hearing the noise, the family woke up and rushed into the garden.

They were amazed by what they saw.

In the corner of the garden were two burglars curled into balls.

Chief stood over them growling.

The whole garden was lit up with the glow from Twinkletoes' feet.

Dad phoned the police and they took the burglars to jail.

Mum said, 'How strange! The garden seems to be glowing!'

The children both squealed,
'Look! Look!
There's a fairy
in our garden!'

'I can't see a fairy,'
said Mum.

Twinkletoes sat smiling
on Chief's shoulders
and waved to the children.

20

Thank you for reading my book.

If your child has enjoyed reading 'Twinkletoes' please consider leaving a review.

Printed in Great Britain
by Amazon